For Kristie

Library of Congress catalog card number: 93-73033
Published simultaneously in Canada
by HarperCollins*CanadaLtd*
Color separations by Hong Kong Scanner
Printed and bound in the United States of America
by Berryville Graphics
Designed by Lilian Rosenstreich
First edition, 1994
Second printing, 1994

A TOOTH FAIRY'S TALE

David Christiana

Farrar Straus Giroux New York

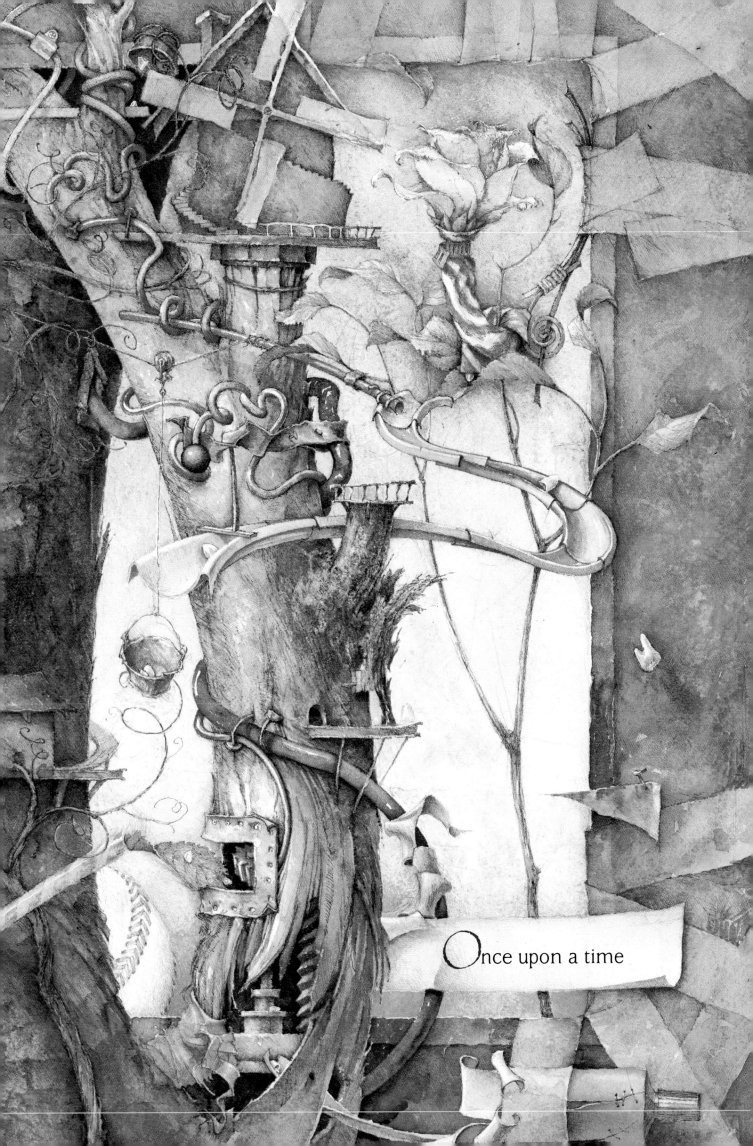

Once upon a time

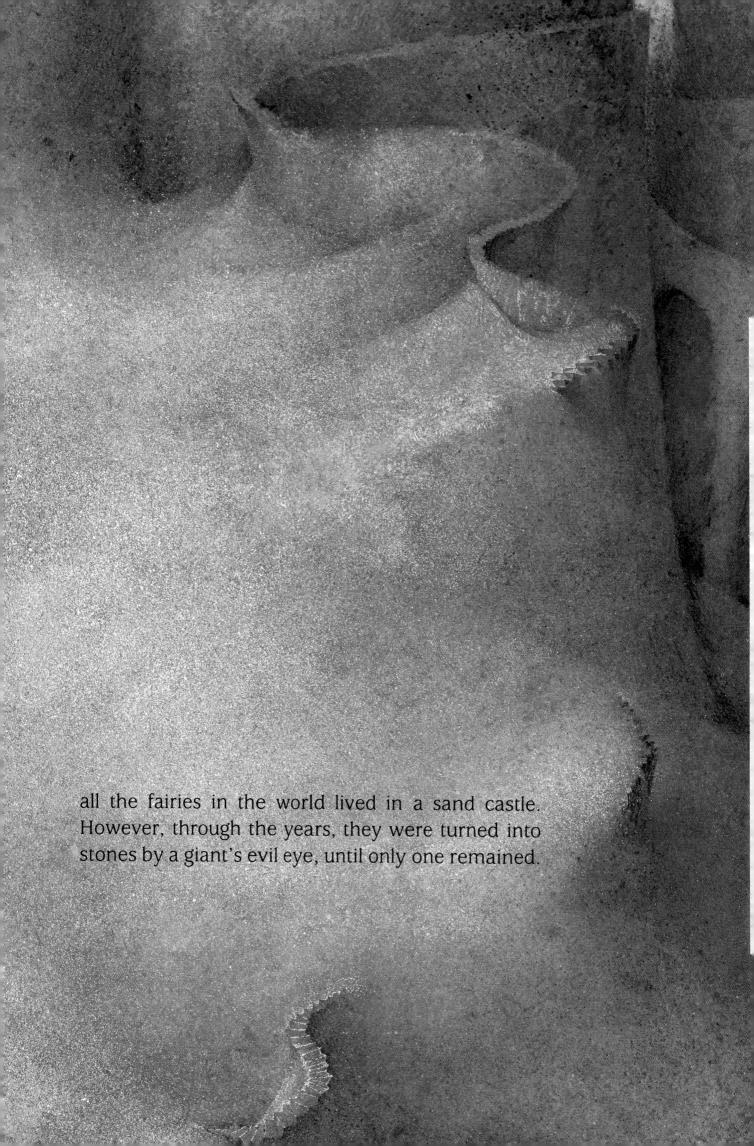

all the fairies in the world lived in a sand castle. However, through the years, they were turned into stones by a giant's evil eye, until only one remained.

She was a Tooth Fairy and she lived in the castle
with her father, the Sandman.

The Sandman's job was to clean the giant's eyes. He used tooth dust for soap and scrubbed each eye with the end of a feather.

The Tooth Fairy's job was to collect baby teeth. When she found one under the giant's pillow, she replaced it with a prize. Sour teeth were chopped up into sand. The rest were made into tooth dust.

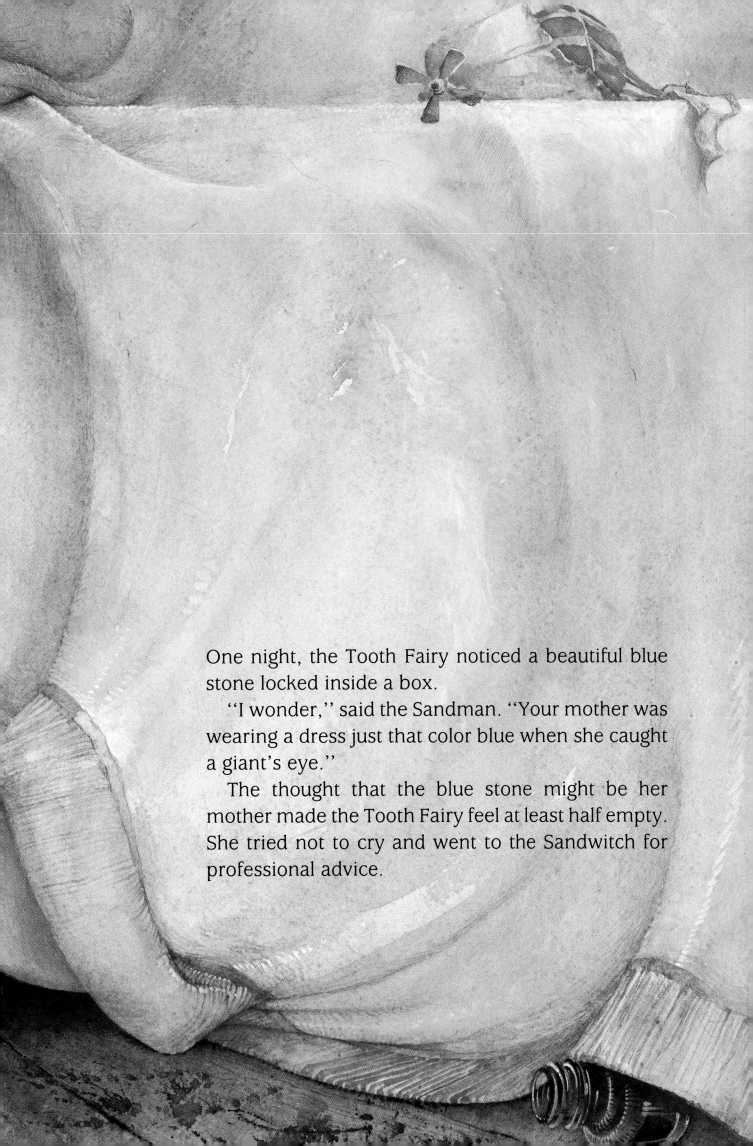

One night, the Tooth Fairy noticed a beautiful blue stone locked inside a box.

"I wonder," said the Sandman. "Your mother was wearing a dress just that color blue when she caught a giant's eye."

The thought that the blue stone might be her mother made the Tooth Fairy feel at least half empty. She tried not to cry and went to the Sandwitch for professional advice.

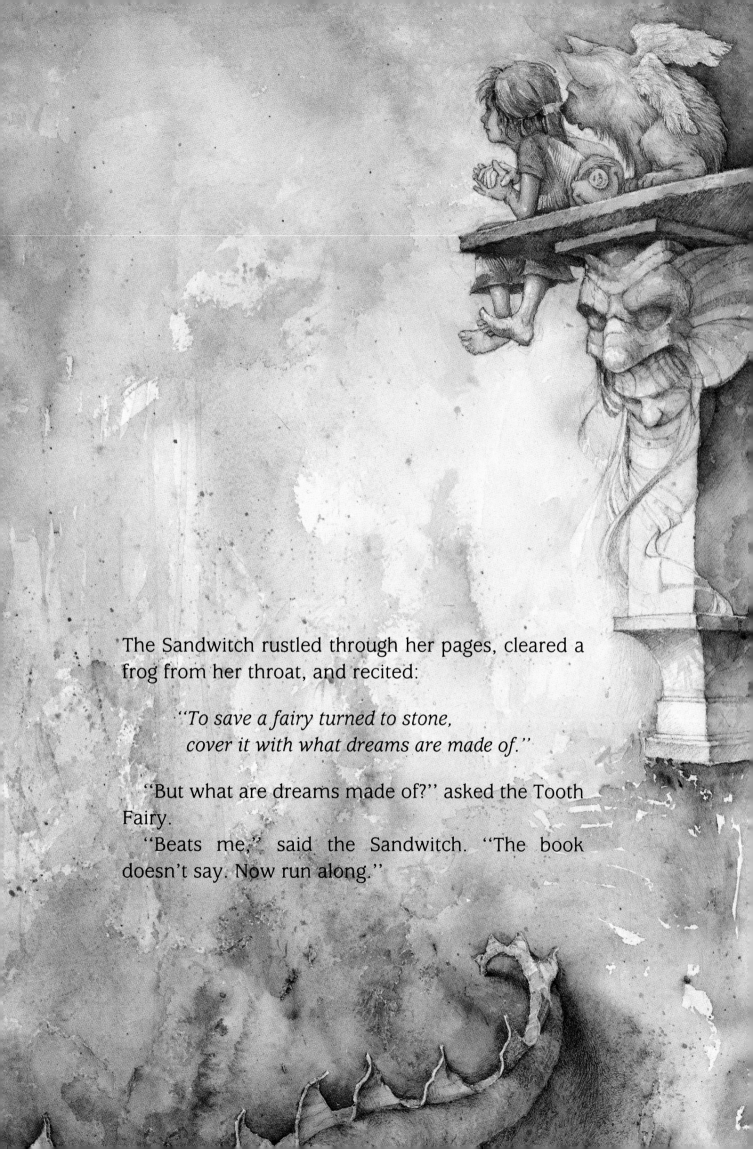

The Sandwitch rustled through her pages, cleared a frog from her throat, and recited:

> *"To save a fairy turned to stone,*
> *cover it with what dreams are made of."*

"But what are dreams made of?" asked the Tooth Fairy.

"Beats me," said the Sandwitch. "The book doesn't say. Now run along."

So, the next night, the Tooth Fairy took matters into her own hands and wrote a note to the sleeping giant:

> *Dear Giant, sir,*
> *   May I buy your fine blue stone?*
> *   Thank you very much,*
> *   The Tooth Fairy*

When the giant saw the note, at first he said, "Of course, if she will pay seven cents." But then he thought again. "What if she'd pay a dime, or a dollar, or a million?"

He left a note of his own:

> *Dearest Delightful Fairy,*
> *   It is a lovely stone indeed.*
> *If you give me <u>all</u> your money,*
> *   the precious stone is yours.*
> *   The Giant*

The Tooth Fairy gave the giant all her money and wrote a letter back:

Dear Giant,
    Please, leave the stone under your
    pillow tonight.

                            Thank you,
                            The Tooth Fairy

The next morning, when the giant saw the money, he said, "What a deal!" But then he reconsidered. "If she had that much money, I bet she has a lot of stuff. And she does like that stone." He wrote another note:

Dear Tooth Fairy,
    Thanks for the money, but it just isn't enough.
Give me something special that money can't buy.
Then, I swear, the stone is yours.

                            The Giant

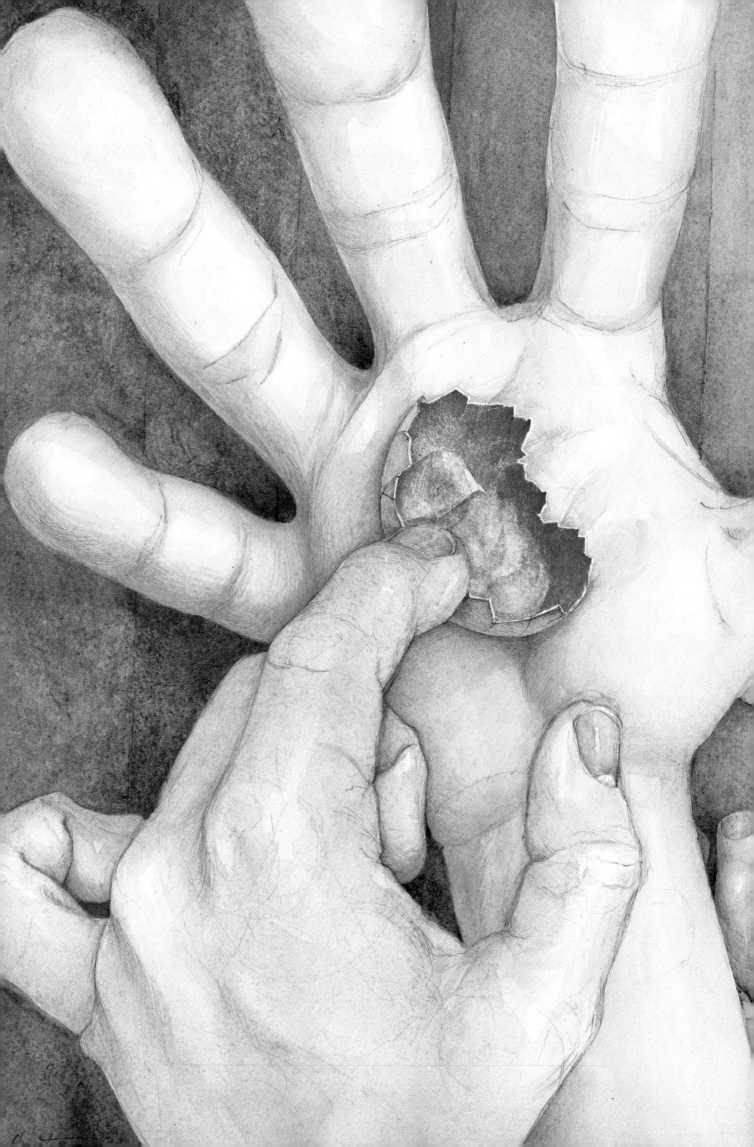

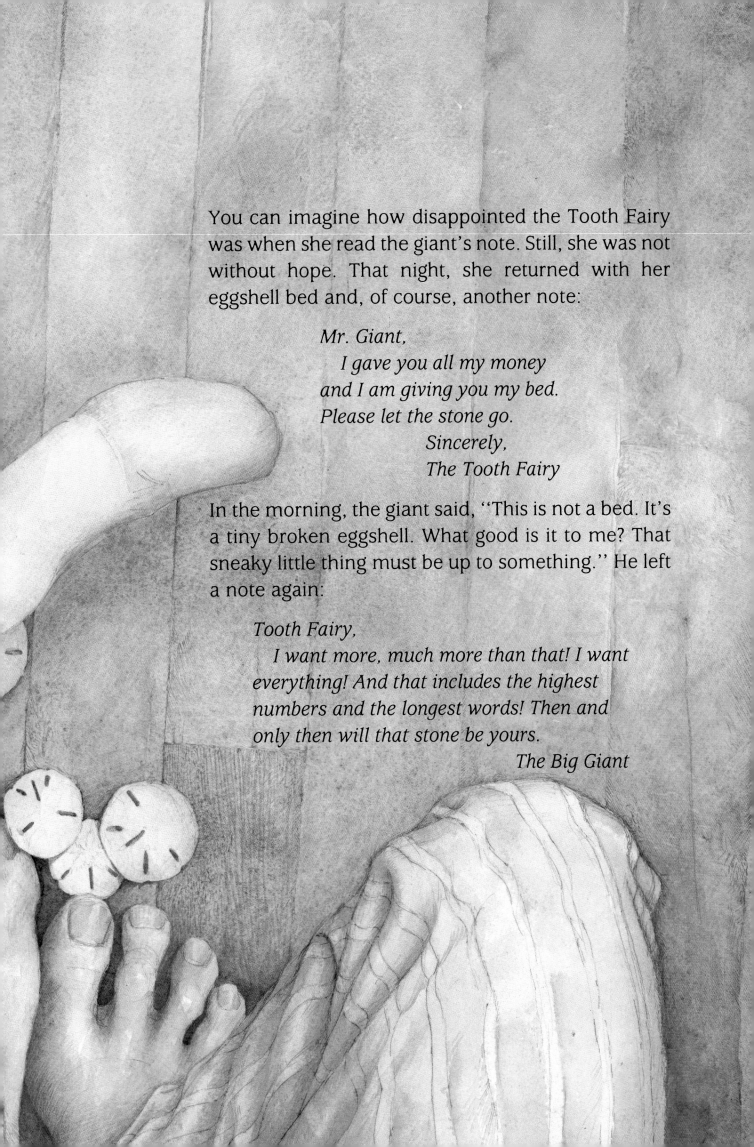

You can imagine how disappointed the Tooth Fairy was when she read the giant's note. Still, she was not without hope. That night, she returned with her eggshell bed and, of course, another note:

> Mr. Giant,
>   I gave you all my money
> and I am giving you my bed.
> Please let the stone go.
>   Sincerely,
>   The Tooth Fairy

In the morning, the giant said, "This is not a bed. It's a tiny broken eggshell. What good is it to me? That sneaky little thing must be up to something." He left a note again:

> Tooth Fairy,
>   I want more, much more than that! I want
> everything! And that includes the highest
> numbers and the longest words! Then and
> only then will that stone be yours.
>   The Big Giant

At first, she was confused, but when she thought it through, the Tooth Fairy knew where to find the highest numbers and the longest words. A book on mathematics and an enormous dictionary were delivered to the giant, along with a note:

> *Giant:*
> *You promised me that stone!*
> *Please.*
>
>   *T.F.*

The giant wrote back:

T.F.
OKAY! The stone is yours.
See you tomorrow night.
THE GREAT BIG GIANT

When the Tooth Fairy and the Sandman returned the following night, they found that the stone was no longer in the box.

"Don't touch it!" the Sandman whispered. "The giant set a trap. If you move the stone, he might wake up and see you. Then you'll end up as a stone."

That night, the Sandman did not clean the giant's eyes. Instead, he sealed them shut with toothpaste. Then the Tooth Fairy grabbed the stone.

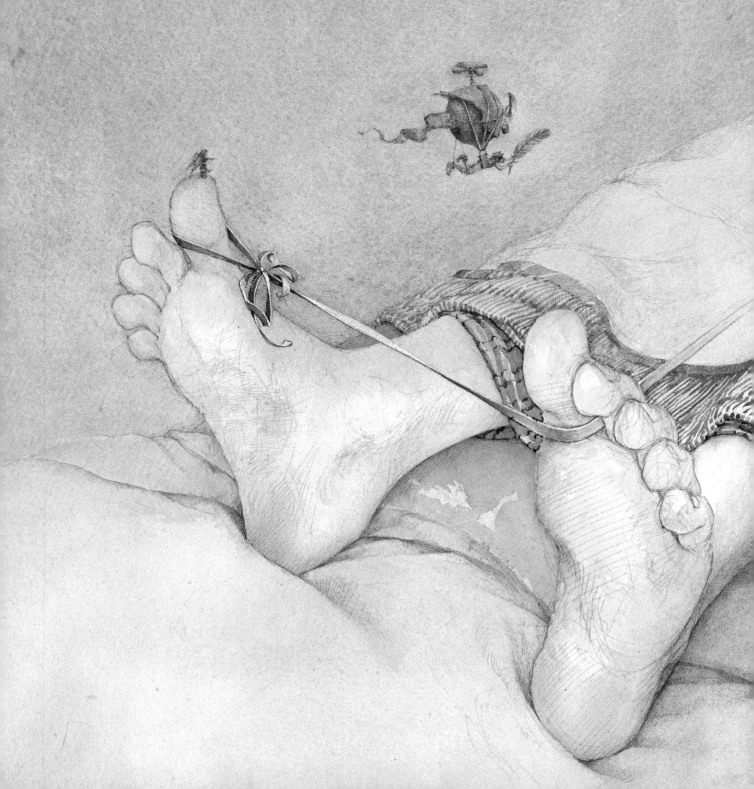

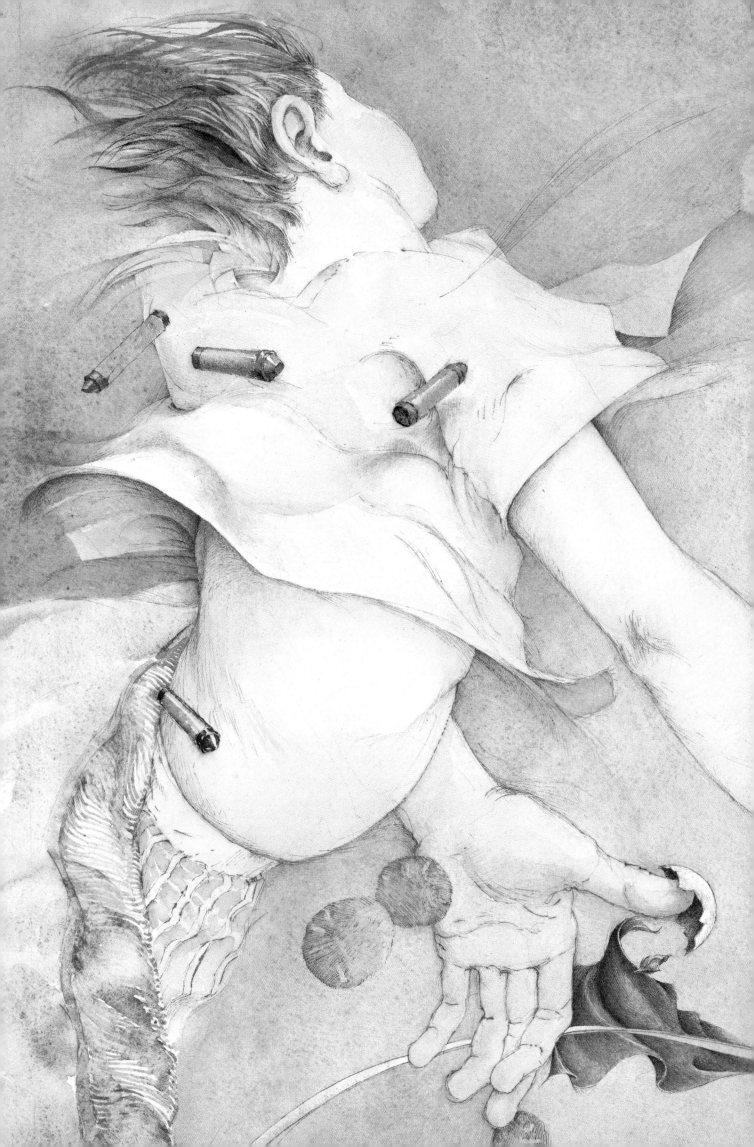

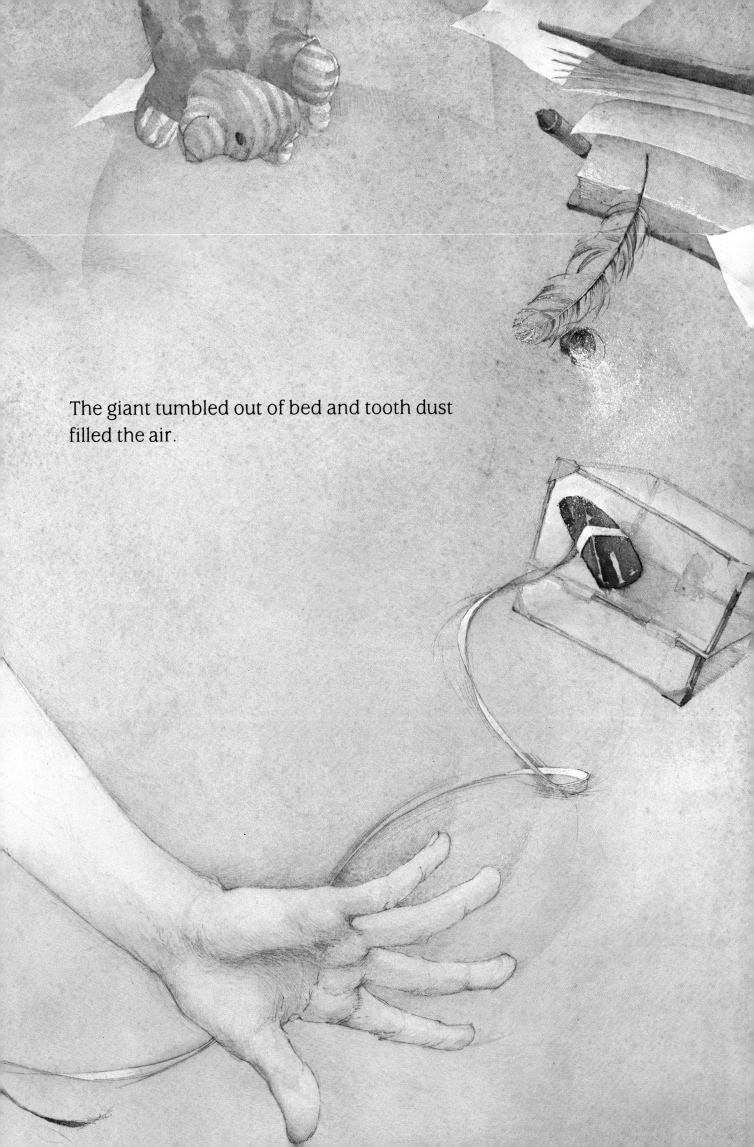

The giant tumbled out of bed and tooth dust
filled the air.

It settled on the stone like clean white snow, and the giant's spell was broken. The Tooth Fairy's mother appeared with a smile, and each of their hearts had never felt so full.

And, having learned that dreams are made of tooth dust, they lived happily ever after.

Except for the giant, who, at times, has sour dreams.